Bob

Barbara

John Steinbeck was **Wrong** about **O**klahoma!

BY

BOB BURKE

OKLAHOMA HERITAGE ASSOCIATION
2008 BOARD OF DIRECTORS

My hat is off to Bob Burke for saying emphatically in 2008 what I tried to say some 50 years ago as a member of the Oklahoma House of Representatives—John Steinbeck was wrong! The image Steinbeck gave us—that Oklahoma was the only state in the Dust Bowl—still haunts me.

As governor, I had opportunities to travel the world promoting Oklahoma and its products. I will never forget a night in Hong Kong when the chairman of the largest financial institution in the Far East was hosting our delegation.

He was late and went directly to the microphone when he arrived. He opened his remarks with, "All I know about Oklahoma is what I have read in *The Grapes of Wrath*."

I cringed and remembered the day in 1957 during the Oklahoma semi-centennial celebration when I took "personal privilege" to address my fellow members of the legislature and offered a resolution to withdraw the official invitation to have John Steinbeck as our guest of honor.

I don't remember my words, but the *Chronicles of Oklahoma* quotes me as saying, "He has done more to create a stench…against us than anything else!" The invitation was withdrawn, but the image lingers on. The image is wrong and Steinbeck was wrong.

George Nigh
Former Governor of Oklahoma

4

THE *GREAT* DEBATE

I take this opportunity to debate the magnificent American author, John Steinbeck, on the attributes of an "Okie." Steinbeck died in 1968, but I will refute his everlasting words that have painted the stereotypical picture of an Oklahoman. I will go far beyond his mythical Joad family and relate the accomplishments of Oklahomans whose ideas have changed the world in our state's first century.

Oklahomans were nothing like the families that Steinbeck portrayed as idealess, shiftless, hick tenant farmers in *The Grapes of Wrath* in 1939. Steinback won the Pulitzer Price for the book, but he had never set foot in Oklahoma before he wrote the story. Unfortunately, the images Steinback painted of Oklahomans trying to escape the ravages of the Great Depression negatively influenced opinions about the quality of the people of Oklahoma.

There is no doubt that Oklahoma suffered in the Great Depression. The longest and most severe economic downturn in modern history caused oil to plummet to 20 cents a barrel, closed mines and businesses, and resulted in thousands of farm and other property foreclosures. Dust storms ravaged some areas of western Oklahoma as drought-stricken soil was lifted into the sky, often darkening the entire horizon. The dust blew in such quantity that trains stopped, airports closed, and chickens went to roost at noon in the darkness.

Many Oklahomans were forced to leave for California where jobs were more plentiful. The real-life story caused Steinback to pick the eastern Oklahoma town of Sallisaw to set his novel for the Joad family heading west. Steinbeck's words gave the nation its enduring symbol of human misery and the migrants an unforgettable badge of shame.

Steinback labeled Oklahomans as "scum." He wrote dialogue between the characters:

> *Well, Okie use' ta mean you was from Oklahoma.*
> *Now it means you're a dirty son-of-a-bitch. Okie*
> *means you're scum. Don't mean nothing itself, it's*
> *the way they say it.*

Steinbeck accused Oklahomans of having no grit and determination in the face of trouble. He wrote:

> *Men stood by their fences and looked at the ruined*
> *corn, drying fast now, only a little green showing*
> *through the film of dust. The men were silent and*
> *they did not move often. And the women came out*
> *of the houses to stand by their men...To feel whether*
> *this time the men would break. After awhile, the*
> *faces of the watching men lost their bemused*
> *perplexity and became hard and angry.*

Steinback cast an indelible image that Okies were without resolution and hope:

> *Where'll we go? Where'll we go, the women asked.*
> *We don't know. We don't know. And the women went*
> *quickly, quietly back into the houses and herded the*
> *children ahead of them. They knew that a man so*
> *hurt and so perplexed may turn in anger, even on*
> *people he loves. They left the men alone to figure*
> *and to wonder in the dust.*

I have teamed up in this debate with David L. Boren's father, Lyle H. Boren, the youngest man ever elected to the Congress of the United States. After Steinbeck released *The Grapes of Wrath* in 1939, Boren, representing Oklahoma's old Fourth Congressional District, and himself the son of a tenant farmer, took personal privilege on the floor of the United States House of Representatives and blistered Steinbeck and his book:

> *The painting Steinbeck made in his book is a lie… a damnable lie, a black, infernal creation of a twisted, distorted mind. Though I regret that there is a mind in America such as his, let it be a matter of record for all the tenant farmers in America that I have denied this lie for them. Take the vulgarity out of this book and it would be blank from cover to cover.* The Grapes of Wrath *that John Steinbeck would father in a world of truth and right would press for him only the bitter drink of just condemnation and isolation for his unclean mind.*

After Lyle's tirade, he convinced the United States Post Office Department that *The Grapes of Wrath* was obscene and unfit for delivery by federal mailmen. For more than a year, shipment of the book was banned from government mail routes.

If Steinbeck had visited Oklahoma before, during, and after the Great Depression, he would have found a thriving group of leaders whose ideas would change the world around them. He would have seen that Oklahomans were more than just honest, hard-working tillers of the land that had been scarred by drought and conditions; he would have been surrounded by a sophisticated band of the leading minds of the day. He also would find Oklahomans were filled with grit and determination—unwilling to allow any natural or man-made disaster to derail their ambitions.

My case in chief for proving Steinbeck's image of Oklahomans to be wrong is couched in a review of ideas that Oklahomans have given to the world in our state's first 100 years.

Oklahomans always have had great ideas. Innovations that changed the American way of life came from men and women in Oklahoma who dared to dream beyond confining lines drawn by custom and tradition.

Most students of Oklahoma history are familiar with some legendary and unique inventions and achievements. S.N. Goldman invented the shopping cart and changed life forever. Carl Magee teamed up with engineers from Oklahoma A & M and designed the first parking meter. Wiley Post was the first person to fly solo around the world.

In addition to the oft-told stories of inventing shopping carts and parking meters and flying around the world, the dreams of many other Oklahomans have improved the quality and enjoyment of life in a multitude of venues, from literature to commerce to civil rights. Some ideas took the form of the written word—while others emanated from engineering drawings and test tubes.

The world's first parking meter was invented by Oklahoma City newspaperman Carl Magee. It was installed in downtown Oklahoma City and changed the way America controlled parking along city streets in retail shopping districts.

From an early age, Gary England wanted to be a television weather forecaster. Not only did he succeed in becoming the state's best-known weatherman, his technological innovations to warn residents of approaching storms have been adopted around the world.

Someone once said, "Necessity is the mother of invention." That theory has been oft-proved in Oklahoma. When howling winds and searing drought removed valuable topsoil from western Oklahoma during the Great Depression, it was Oklahoma conservationists who planned and built America's first shelterbelt of trees to protect the land from the elements. L.A. Macklanburg invented and patented weather stripping after his wife grew frustrated because the prairie wind constantly blew dust around the front door into her new home.

Damaging floodwaters necessitated the building of upstream dams to impound water before it could inundate cropland. It was in Oklahoma where the nation's first upstream dam-flood protection plan was implemented. Oklahoma's location in the tornado-prone plains resulted in meteorologist Gary England's innovations that now are common tools worldwide in weather forecasting. England developed First Warning, a severe weather warning system that appears on maps in the corner of the television screen.

Consumer wants and needs spawned ideas in Oklahoma. Phillips Petroleum scientists invented the aerosol can and plastic in Bartlesville. Who can imagine American life without spray cans and thousands of plastic products that we use daily?

The Ditch Witch trenching machine replaced the pick and shovel in digging trenches for utility lines. The machine was the idea of machine shop owner Ed Malzahn. The idea for mud flaps on trucks, to prevent the wheels of big rigs from kicking up mud and rocks, came from Oscar March, a long-haul driver at Tinker Air Force Base in Midwest City.

Ed Malzahn spent nights and weekends in his machine shop in Perry drawing, producing, and testing what became the Ditch Witch trenching machine. Ditch Witch is an icon in its field around the world.

Angie Debo is arguably Oklahoma's greatest historian. She was courageous in writing the truth about exploitation of Native Americans. Her works have been cited by other historians around the world. If John Steinbeck would have visited Oklahoma, he no doubt would have come in contact with Debo, a premier historical researcher.

Charles Banks Wilson's portrait of Will Rogers—Oklahoma's favorite son. At the height of his popularity, Rogers was a giant movie star and the most-read newspaper columnist in the country.

Ralph Ellison grew up in a poor neighborhood in northeast Oklahoma City. He wanted to be a trumpet player, but was attracted to writing. His *Invisible Man* is a classic in American literature.

In Oklahoma's first century, true Oklahoma wordsmiths recorded history in voluminous fashion. Marquis James won Pulitzer Prizes for biographies of Sam Houston and Andrew Jackson. Grant Foreman wrote of the American West, including the great trails that crossed Oklahoma. Angie Debo courageously preserved the story of a difficult time of transition for the state's Native American population. John Hope Franklin became the nation's leading African American historian. Their ideas of chronicling the past made a huge impact on how historians would record the occurrences of succeeding decades.

Oklahoma fiction writers filled the wish lists of America's readers with romance, science fiction, the Old West, and mystery. After growing up in poverty in northeast Oklahoma City, Ralph Ellison wrote *Invisible Man*, considered one of the top five novels in American history, the first book written from the perspective of an African American.

Gene Autry was not only a pioneer singing cowboy, but also was a gifted songwriter. His brand of bringing music to western movies changed the industry forever.

Louis L'Amour wrote more than 100 fiction masterpieces about the Old West. N. Scott Momaday, Tony Hillerman, Billie Letts, S.E. Hinton, Carolyn Hart, and Joyce Carol Thomas have produced some of America's finest literary works. Some have been translated into other languages, while others have been made into major movies.

Actor James Garner was born James Baumgardner in Norman. He carved for himself a unique place in Hollywood, branding for himself roles in television shows and dozens of movies.

Savoie Lottinville transformed the University of Oklahoma Press into a well-respected publisher. Daniel J. Boorstin not only wrote 20 books, but served as the Librarian of Congress.

Staying with ideas of culture, innovative Oklahomans have embellished movies, television, ballet, and music. Our favorite son, Will Rogers, bridged the gap between vaudeville and the silver screen. Gene Autry, Dale Robertson, James Garner, Megan Mullally, Kristin

Chenoweth, Van Heflin, Shirley Jones, Alfre Woodard, Brad Pitt, Tony Randall, and Chuck Norris have contributed their unique acting styles to movie and television productions. Grey Frederickson won an Oscar for producing one of the Godfather movies. Duncan's Ron Howard continues to direct and produce major motion pictures.

Te Ata Fisher, the famous Chickasaw storyteller, thrilled presidents, royalty, and the common man with her dramatic interpretations of Native American folklore. Five Oklahoma Native American ballerinas, Yvonne Chouteau, Rosella Hightower, Moscelyne Larkin, Maria Tallchief, and Marjorie Tallchief, are considered among the superstars of the ballet stage of the twentieth century. Leona Mitchell has thrilled opera audiences all over the world.

Mike Larsen's mural of Oklahoma ballerinas is in the rotunda of the Oklahoma State Capitol. From our frontier state came five Native American ballerinas who stunned audiences around the world.

Woody Guthrie was an Oklahoma singer and songwriter unequaled in his field. Contemporary performers such as Bob Dylan attribute their musical leanings to Guthrie's style of folk music.

Reba McEntire has won almost every award in the American country music industry. Hailing from a small community in southeast Oklahoma, she made it to the big time with a unique talent.

    Woody Guthrie and Bob Wills put their unique stamps on the American music scene. Both influenced dozens of later stars with their special brand of lyrics and music. Wills literally created a new style of music and Guthrie wrote one of history's most-recorded songs, "This Land is Your Land." Gene Autry gave the world "Santa Claus is Coming to Town" and "Rudolph the Red-Nosed Reindeer."

    Oklahomans fill the pages of *Who's Who in American Music* with legendary songwriters Jimmy Webb, whose songs made stars of singers such as Glen Campbell and The Fifth Dimension, and Mae Boren Axton, my high school English teacher, who wrote Elvis Presley's first hit, "Heartbreak Hotel." Oklahoma performers include Patti Page, Roger Miller, Garth Brooks, Toby Keith, Reba McEntire, Carrie Underwood, Wayne Coyne of the Flaming Lips, Michael Hedges, and Vince Gill.

Deep Deuce on Northeast Second Street in Oklahoma City produced jazz legends such as Jimmy Rushing and Charlie Christian, a young man who is credited with adding the electric guitar as a solo instrument in jazz. Both stars were guided by a novel music teacher, Zelia Breaux, at Douglass High School in Oklahoma City. Her ideas influenced an entire generation of musical artists.

Professor Oscar Jacobson at the University of Oklahoma tutored five young Kiowa art students whose artistic endeavors as the Kiowa Five transformed Native American art. Apache Alan Houser became one of the nation's leading sculptors and Charles Banks Wilson won international acclaim for his paintings. His portraits of Jim Thorpe, Sequoyah, Robert S. Kerr, and Will Rogers majestically hang in the rotunda of the State Capitol.

Woodrow Crumbo, a Pottawatomie, and Jerome Tiger are considered among the elite of the country's Native American artists. Acee Blue Eagle, a Creek-Pawnee artist, was the first Native American artist to embark on a solo career, traveling worldwide to promote Indian art.

Oklahoma country music superstar Toby Keith took his style of country music from nightclubs to record-breaking albums.

An example of the forward-thinking attitude of Oklahomans is Zelia Breux. As a high school music teacher, she influenced a generation of African American musicians and performers, including Ralph Ellison, Charlie Christian, and Jimmy Rushing.

Wilson Hurley's masterpieces gracing the great hall at the National Cowboy and Western Heritage Museum are but a hint of his talent. Augusta Metcalfe's paintings have been displayed across the nation. She won a 1911 art competition at the Oklahoma State Fair and focused her entire life's work on painting Oklahoma life and landscapes. Mike Wimmer leads a new generation of artists whose works garner national and international awards. These Oklahoma artists' works are held in public and private collections worldwide.

Oklahomans have translated their ideas and observance of life into the written word as poetry. The state has produced many Pulitzer Prize-winning poets, including John Berryman and N. Scott Momaday, selected to pen the poem that would officially be sanctioned to celebrate Oklahoma's Centennial in 2007.

BELOW: Dr. Nazih Zuhdi's innovations revolutionized the heart transplant procedure. His medical breakthrough allowed transplants to become a viable option for people who otherwise would not survive.

ABOVE: N. Scott Momaday is an Oklahoma Pulitzer Prize-winning poet. Momaday's writings of his Native American heritage are considered of the highest quality by critics worldwide.

While some Oklahomans' ideas improved the quality or enjoyment of life, Oklahoma scientists and medical professionals improved life itself. Dr. Nazih Zuhdi's development of a procedure to prime the heart-lung machine opened the gateway to heart transplants. Dr. Donald O'Donoghue was known through the nation for his knee surgery techniques. As a United States Army doctor in a field hospital during World War II, Dr. Henry Freede treated the world's first quadruple amputation victim, a young man whose limbs had been splintered by enemy fire. Dr. Clyde Snow perfected the science of osteobiography. He is without peer in the world of identification and analysis of bones.

In 1965, Oklahoma City leaders Stanton L. Young, Dean McGee, Harvey Everest, E.K. Gaylord, and Dr. O'Donoghue founded the Oklahoma Health Center south of the State Capitol. The 300-acre complex now is home to 30 member organizations ranging from cutting-edge biotechnology companies to government, education, patient care, and community support institutions. Life-changing health care and research is concentrated within an area of a few square blocks and literally is on the frontier of health care in the modern world.

Researchers at the Oklahoma Medical Research Foundation have produced many life-improving breakthroughs. Dr. Petar Alaupovic created a naming and classification system for certain proteins that became the international standard. Dr. Robert Nordquist developed a strain of breast cancer cells that helped researchers better understand tumors. Dr. Fletcher Taylor and Dr. Charles Esmon pioneered work that resulted in the first treatment for a deadly blood infection in children. Dr. Esmon was recognized as one of the premier cardiovascular biologists in the world. One of the drugs he developed, Ceprotin, was the first drug ever approved under the European Union's centralized licensing procedure.

Dr. John Harley and Judith James made waves in the world of biomedical research by pinpointing the genetic and environmental triggers for lupus. Dr. Robert Floyd and Dr. Rheal Towner have made breakthroughs in research that hopefully will produce a compound that can serve as an effective weapon against brain and liver cancer. In 2000, Dr. Jordan Tang and his team at the Oklahoma Medical Research Foundation identified the enzyme responsible for Alzheimer's disease and continues research that will someday create help for those stricken with the condition. Dr. William Canfield and his company have developed new technologies for manufacturing enzymes. World-class biotechnology research is being conducted by many companies and organizations in Oklahoma.

Dr. J.V.D. Hough founded the Hough Ear Institute, the world's only ear institute to contribute to the research and invention of all four major breakthroughs in hearing medicine—cochlear implants for profound and total deafness, implantable devices for nerve deafness, implantable devices for conductive deafness, and standard hearing aids for less affluent countries.

Lester and John Sabolich became internationally famous for breakthrough prosthetic designs such as the Sabolich Socket. Dr. Kenneth Cooper literally invented the word "aerobics." His plan for physical fitness has endured for two generations.

Oklahoma has become a world leader in bioinformatics, the emerging science of using sophisticated computer processes and software to analyze data arising from the mapping of the human genome. Scientists in Oklahoma have made great strides in research into diabetes-related conditions and the development of diagnostic and therapeutic products for viral diseases. ProteomTech, an Oklahoma City company, was the world's first company to commercially manufacture human proteins that can be turned into life-saving drugs. The Dean A. McGee Eye Institute is one of the largest ophthalmology institutes in the nation.

The world of space has benefited from the brainpower of Oklahomans. In fact, no other state can claim the vast influence upon space exploration. Wiley Post was not only the first person to solo around the planet, but he discovered the jet stream and developed a pressurized flying suit, the forerunner of the modern space suit.

Oklahoma astronaut Tom Stafford created his place in history by bringing together the two leading nations of the world, the United States and the Soviet Union, in exploring space.

John Herrington combined his proud Chickasaw heritage and a brilliant mind to become a leading astronaut in America's space program.

LEFT: Mike Wimmer's portrait of aviation hero Wiley Post hangs in the State Capitol. Post overcame great odds, including a severe depression problem and the loss of an eye, to become the world's greatest pilot. This self-taught scientist perhaps was the most popular person in the world in 1933 as the first person to fly solo around the Earth.

Colonel Jack Ridley was the test pilot and project engineer who made it possible for the sound barrier to be broken in 1947. Jerrie Cobb was among the elite of women pilots who prepared America for the space age. Leroy Gordon Cooper was chosen in the first group of American astronauts. The first director of NASA was James Webb, an Oklahoman whose voice for space exploration was loudly heard. Shannon Lucid was among the first women selected in the American space program.

Thomas Stafford paved the way for the lunar landing with his command of *Apollo 10* and made history by pioneering joint space projects between the United States and the Soviet Union. John Herrington was the first Native American astronaut in the space program. Donna Shirley was the project manager for the innovative exploration of the planet Mars with a robotic rover.

BELOW: John W. Nichols was a young accountant in Oklahoma City when he changed the way oil and gas drilling was funded around the globe. He and his son, Larry, founded the state's largest public company, Devon Energy Corporation.

ABOVE: Jeane Kirkpatrick appeared on the cover of *The Saturday Evening Post*. As one of the world's most respected leaders, she opened the doors for women in government.

Oklahomans' ideas have improved education, both in Oklahoma and the nation. Henry Bennett was without peer in advancing new educational ideas in the nation's agricultural and mechanical colleges. Francis Tuttle's ideas in the field of vocational-technical education were duplicated by many states. David Boren's systematic approach at raising funds at public universities will be studied and mimicked for generations.

Ideas have catapulted Oklahomans onto the national political stage. Carl Albert was Speaker of the United States House of Representatives; Patrick Hurley was Secretary of War in the Herbert Hoover administration; Bryce Harlow held cabinet-level positions in the Dwight Eisenhower and Richard Nixon administrations; Robert S. Kerr was the uncrowned king of the United States Senate; and David Boren chaired the Senate's Intelligence Committee longer than anyone else in history.

Oklahoma women have contributed their ideas of leadership on the world stage. Wilma Mankiller, when elected chief of the Cherokee Nation, was the first woman to head a major Native American tribal government. Jeane Kirkpatrick was appointed by President Ronald Reagan as the first female United States Ambassador to the United Nations. Alice Robertson was the second woman elected to Congress and the first woman to preside over the House of Representatives. Kate Barnard was the first woman in the nation elected to a statewide political, non-education office.

The world of commerce has benefited greatly from the ideas of Oklahomans. Erle P. Halliburton pawned his wife's wedding ring to finance a new idea of using a measuring line to assist in the cementing of oil and gas wells. That idea birthed Halliburton, one of the world's largest companies. Charles Gould, the "father of Oklahoma geology," developed techniques for discovering many oil and gas fields in the region.

John W. Nichols, a young accountant, won approval of the first oil and gas funding proposal formally approved by the Securities and Exchange Commission. That idea changed the way that worldwide oil and gas production was financed. Nichols and his son, Larry, founded the state's largest publicly-traded company, Devon Energy Corporation.

Bill Swisher and CMI Corporation designed a new road-building material spreader and grader that revolutionized the industry. In a garage apartment in north Oklahoma City, Herman Meinders founded what is now Teleflora, the world's largest flowers-by-wire service. The twisty-tie, used to keep bread fresh and plastic bags sealed, was invented near Maysville. Chase Beider developed a process to copy documents and was instrumental in the founding of the company that now is known as Xerox.

The petroleum-rich history of the state produced idea leaders who made fortunes from pulling crude and gas from beneath the surface. The names associated with Oklahoma are the most famous in world petroleum history. J. Paul Getty and T. Boone Pickens became two of the world's richest men. Harry Sinclair founded the Sinclair Oil Company. The company that became Conoco began in the oilfields of Osage County by Governor E.W. Marland.

Robert S. Kerr and Dean McGee joined forces to create a giant in the petroleum industry, Kerr-McGee Corporation. Kerr-McGee was the first company to sink an oil well offshore. Frank and L.E. Phillips leased oil-rich lands from the Osage Indians and founded Phillips Petroleum Company. In recent years, Aubrey McClendon has vaulted his Chesapeake Energy Corporation into a major player in America's energy industry. The Williams Companies built the nation's first coal-slurry, hydrogen-sulfide, and anhydrous ammonia pipelines. When pipelines were no longer being used to transport petroleum, Williams engineers pioneered the use of pipelines as conduits for fiber-optic cable. Callidus Tech developed a high-pressure flare tip for the oil and gas industry.

The Pioneer Woman Statue was E.W. Marland's gift to the people of Ponca City. Marland also was largely responsible for the creation of the Interstate Oil Compact Commission.

Bob Funk's desire to help people find jobs, and his ideas of implementing his dream and giving people hope, has resulted in Express Personnel Services becoming one of the nation's largest staffing agencies, with offices from Oklahoma to Russia. Ray Ackerman employed advertising ideas learned as an ad salesman for *The Daily Oklahoman* to Ackerman McQueen, one of the nation's premier advertising agencies with clients around the world.

Lee Allan Smith became one of the country's leading promoters and expediters of civic ideas and celebrations. The commercial ideas of Edward L. Gaylord expanded beyond ownership of the state's largest newspaper. The Gaylord family influence spread into the broadcasting and entertainment industry, including ownership of the Grand Ole Opry.

George Kaiser expanded his family's fortune with innovative entrepreneurial ideas and became the most financially successful Oklahoman. Another Tulsan, Henry Kravis, became a titan of American finance and founded one of the nation's leading private equity firms. Harland Stonecipher had a unique idea—to offer customers insurance to cover unexpected legal fees. Pre-Paid Legal Services is the largest insurer of its kind in the world. The idea for Integrated Medical Delivery was formed in Oklahoma. The system provides back-office services to health care clients.

Robert S. Kerr was the first governor of Oklahoma to be born in what would become the 46th state. His vision of development of Oklahoma's natural resources, particularly its water, is legendary.

The National Weather Center in Norman is one of the world's most important facilities for weather research and development. *Courtesy Robert Fritchie and the University of Oklahoma.*

Other Oklahoma ideas have created legends. Cyrus Avery provided the architectural genius that birthed the construction of Route 66, a paved highway from Chicago, Illinois, to Los Angeles, California. More than 400 miles of the "Mother Road," featuring drive-in theaters, neon-lighted diners, and rustic trading posts crossed Oklahoma.

Robert S. Kerr's vision of capturing and effectively using Oklahoma water resulted in the construction of the McClellan-Kerr Arkansas River Navigation Project, a system that links Tulsa's Port of Catoosa to the Gulf of Mexico and world trade.

It takes more than good looks to become Miss America—it takes brains and ideas. Oklahoma has produced six Miss Americas, beginning with Norma Smallwood in 1926. Since Jane Jayroe won the crown in 1967, Susan Powell, Shawntel Smith, Jennifer Berry, and Lauren Nelson have proudly worn the prestigious crown.

The world of sports has been influenced by the ideas and performances of Oklahomans. Jim Thorpe was named the world's greatest athlete of the first half of the 20th century. The rodeo sport of bulldogging was invented by African American cowboy Bill Pickett on the 101 Ranch. Oklahoma State University basketball coach Henry P. Iba created the "swinging gate" defense. At the University of Oklahoma, Coach Charles "Bud" Wilkinson introduced the Split-T formation in football and Barry Switzer perfected the Wishbone offense.

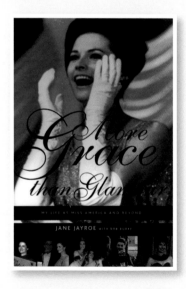

Jane Jayroe's life story was told in her 2006 autobiography, *More Grace Than Glamour*, published by the Oklahoma Heritage Association.

Ten percent of the men who have played major league baseball in America since the game's invention have come through Oklahoma, having been born here, played minor league, sandlot, or college baseball in the state, or having died in Oklahoma. The names of Mickey Mantle, Dizzy Dean, Carl Hubbell, Johnny Bench, Allie Reynolds, Lloyd and Paul Waner, Willie Stargell, Joe Carter, and Pepper Martin are synonymous with baseball history.

Jim Thorpe recently was selected as the sixth-greatest college football player of all time. He was the first president of the National Football League.

BELOW: After Babe Ruth, many baseball fans believe that Mickey Mantle is the greatest and best known major leaguer in history. Mantle, left, and Allie Reynolds, both native Oklahomans, are two of the New York Yankees' greatest players.

Clayton I. Bennett owns Oklahoma City's National Basketball Association franchise and OU graduate, Pat Bowlen, is the principal owner of the Denver Broncos of the National Football League.

There is no greater area in which Oklahoma ideas played a major role as in the struggle for equality. Early Oklahoma cases allowed the United States Supreme Court to strike down laws that prevented African Americans from voting and invalidated local ordinances that forced minorities to live in certain sections of a community. It was an Oklahoma case, spawned by ideas of Oklahoma lawyers, that stopped the practice of excluding African Americans from juries.

Roscoe Dunjee, editor of the *Black Dispatch* in Oklahoma City, was a man of great ideas when it concerned the battle for civil rights. Dunjee hired future United States Supreme Court Justice Thurgood Marshall to represent a young Chickasha girl, Ada Lois Sipuel Fisher, who wanted to attend the all-white University of Oklahoma School of Law. The nation's highest court used the Fisher case to open higher education to minorities across the country. An Oklahoman, Juanita Kidd Stout, was the first African American woman in the nation to be elected a judge.

Clara Luper was an Oklahoma innovator. She led the first sit-down civil rights protests in the South. African American leaders copied her non-violent methods used at downtown Oklahoma City dining establishments and retail stores to break the barriers of segregation.

If John Steinbeck appeared in person in our debate, I would look him in the eye and say, "Mr. Steinbeck, you are a gifted and talented writer. Your way of spinning stories is perhaps without equal. However, you had it wrong about Oklahoma. We have never been afraid of facing problems head-on. That is the Oklahoma spirit!"

Oklahomans always have stood tall in the face of horrible adversity, whether natural disasters such as F-5 tornadoes, or man-made calamities such as the bombing of the Alfred P. Murrah Oklahoma City federal building. That Oklahoma spirit, the ability to rebound from any disaster, is what sets Oklahomans apart from the rest of the world. There is no obstacle that Oklahomans cannot overcome.

The many ideas and accomplishments of Oklahomans that I have used to prove John Steinbeck wrong supports my theory—Oklahoma's incredible story is not about places and things, it is about our people.

It is not about the land runs—although they are unique in world history. Instead, our story is about the pioneers who, at the sound of a rifle or cannon, strode off on horses and bicycles, in wagons, or some jumping from slow-moving trains with a hammer and stake in hand, ready to carve for themselves a new home in a new land.

Oklahoma's story is not about the Trail of Tears, even though that event also is unique in the history of the planet. But, that story is about the many people, some of whom were driven here like animals, who hued for themselves new homes from the forests of eastern Oklahoma.

Oklahoma's incredible story is not about places and events—it is about our people. And, our story will continue to grow in our second century. Mr. Steinbeck, we wish you were alive to sing with us the words of our Centennial song:

WE'RE OKLAHOMA RISING, WE'RE RISING TO BE THE BEST.

Our Incredible State Song

An idea even gave Oklahoma its state song. George Nigh was a 26-year-old high school history teacher in McAlester in 1953 when, as a member of the Oklahoma House of Representatives, he introduced a bill to make the title song from Rodgers and Hammerstein's Broadway play, *Oklahoma!*, the official state song. The move was not without controversy.

Before 1953, the official state song was "Oklahoma (A Toast)," written in 1905 by Harriet Parker Camden. Among the words of the song were, "Oklahoma, fairest daughter of the West, Oklahoma, 'tis the land I love the best."

When George's bill came up for vote, Representative J.W. Huff of Ada stood firmly in opposition to the move. As tears streamed down his face, he said, "I can't believe what you're doing here today. You're going to change a song written by pioneers, steeped in tradition, couched in history. You're going to change it for a song written by two New York Jews who never have even been here and they say 'taters and 'termaters..."

Oklahoma has the most memorable state song of any state in the nation, thanks to the persistence of George Nigh, a young history teacher from McAlester who served his county in the Oklahoma House of Representatives.

Huff left the microphone and walked among fellow members on the House floor as he sang the words of the old song. Everyone in the House chamber rose to their feet as Huff completed the final verse of the old song. George thought his bill was going "down the toilet," but thought quickly of a way to diminish the effect of the emotion. He approached the only microphone at the front podium and said, "Mr. Speaker, I ask unanimous consent to lay this bill over for one legislative day."

With George laying the bill over, Huff and other opponents of the new state song were confident they had won. However, George left the House chamber and went to work. He called Ridge Bond, a fellow McAlesterite and the only Oklahoman to star in the Broadway version of *Oklahoma!* Bond, who played the lead role of Curly, lived in Tulsa at that time. George asked Bond to come to the State Capitol the following day, "prepared to sing."

Next, George called Ira Humprhies, the House member from Chickasha, to invite the choir from the Oklahoma College for Women (OCW) to appear at the Capitol the next day, "provided they know the tunes from Oklahoma!"

The following day George innocently asked unanimous consent to grant privileges to the floor for a special visitor, Bond, the Broadway star, and the OCW Choir. With the House gallery packed, the college choir performed majestically. They sang "Surrey with the Fringe on Top" and "Oh, What a Beautiful Morning." As the pianist began building a dramatic introduction to "Oklahoma," Bond, in his Curly costume, strode to the microphone and brought the house down.

After the rousing rendition of the song, the crowd, including of course the 200 friends and supporters strategically placed there by George, stood and shouted. George took the microphone from Bond and shouted above the melee, "Mr. Speaker, let's do for Oklahoma what Rodgers and Hammerstein did; let's put an exclamation point there. I move we make 'Oklahoma' the state song."

And they did.

OTHER TITLES BY *Bob Burke* INCLUDE

Good Guys Wear White Hats: The Life of George Nigh

Art Treasures of the Oklahoma State Capitol
with Betty Crow and Sandy Meyers

Oklahoma Statesman: The Life of David Boren
with Von Russell Creel

Law & Laughter: The Life of Lee West
with David L. Russell

Al Snipes: Fighter, Founder and Father
with Marshall Snipes

Flowers to Philanthropy: The Life of Herman Meinders
with Tom Butler

A History of the Oklahoma Governor's Mansion
with Betty Crow

Ralph Ellison: A Biography

Lee Allan Smith: Oklahoma's Best Friend
with Gini Moore Campbell

*Simple Truths: The Real Story of the Oklahoma City
Bombing Investigation*
with Jon Hersley and Larry Tongate

Friday Night in the Big Town: The Life of Gary England

A Passion for Equality: The Life of Jimmy Stewart
with Vicki Miles-LaGrange

Old Man River: The Life of Ray Ackerman
with Joan Gilmore

Willie of the Valley: The Life of Bill Paul
with Eric Dabney

Bryce Harlow: Mr. Integrity
with Ralph G. Thompson

OHA   Published by the Oklahoma Heritage Association

31